# Coma

by

David Belbin

Illustrated by Jon Rogers

Published in 2004 in Great Britain by
Barrington Stoke Ltd, Sandeman House, Trunk's Close,
55 High Street, Edinburgh EH1 1SR



ISBN 1-842991-97-3

Printed in Great Britain by Bell & Bain Ltd

Barrington Stoke gratefully acknowledges support from the
Scottish Arts Council towards the publication of the
gr8reads series

# A Note from the Author

I am often asked, "Where do you get your ideas?" I don't know. It's very hard to find good ideas for a story. I was happy when Barrington Stoke sent me a whole lot of stories from the papers. They asked me to choose one and write a short book about it. One of the stories was about a girl in a coma. I chose that one. There are two kinds of coma story. In one the person in the coma wakes up. In the other they don't. Read *Coma* and find out which kind mine is.

For Rhianna

# Contents

# Chapter 1
# My Best Friend's Girl

Todd met Lucy in March.

He was in Year 11. Lucy was in Year 10 at a school on the other side of town. They liked each other from the start.

But Lucy was going out with Todd's best mate, Ben. And Todd was seeing Lucy's friend, Kate. They were all good mates. The 4 of them had lots of laughs.

Then Kate dumped Todd. A week later, Lucy dumped Ben. A week after that, Todd phoned Lucy.

"Do you want to go out?" he asked.

"What took you so long?" she said.

For their first date, they went on a bike ride. They stopped for a burger.

"As soon as I met you I knew Ben was wrong for me," Lucy said.

Todd kissed her long hair. "Kate could see how much I fancied you," he said. "I think that's why she dumped me."

Then they kissed. Then they kissed again. They couldn't keep their hands off each other.

That spring they went on a lot of long walks and bike rides. They rented DVDs and went out for burgers.

Todd knew he had to work for his exams. But he only had time for Lucy.

The exams began. Todd had to work hard. Lucy understood. They only saw each other 2 nights a week. But these were the best nights of their lives. They were getting closer than ever.

One Sunday night, Todd was in his house alone. Lucy came over.

"I love you," she told him in his bedroom.

"I love you, too," he said. "I always will."

"I could never feel this way about any other guy," she said.

It was 10 o'clock. Todd's parents would be back soon. Time for Lucy to go. Todd said he'd cycle home with her.

"Don't be silly," she said. "It's only a 10 minute ride. You need your sleep. Last exam tomorrow."

"Then we can spend all summer together," he said.

"All summer," Lucy agreed. She kissed him again.

She put on her cycle helmet and turned on her lights. Todd watched her cycle off into the dark. He had never been so happy in his life.

# Chapter 2
# Accident

The phone rang at 11 o' clock. Todd's mum picked it up. She talked for a few moments. Then she rushed up the stairs and banged on Todd's door.

"Have you still got Lucy in there?" she asked.

"No," Todd said. "She left an hour ago. What's wrong?"

"That was her mum. Lucy isn't home yet."

"But she must be back by now!" said Todd.

"Her parents think she's still with you," Mum said. "Was she on her bike?"

"Yes," Todd said. "I should never have let her go on her own."

"Maybe she had a flat tyre," Mum said.

"No," Todd told her. "She'd call her parents on her mobile."

Todd got dressed. Mum spoke to Mrs Brown, Lucy's mum. Todd's dad got the car out. They drove out to look for her.

Lucy had been on a well-lit road. There was even a cycle path. But there was no trace of her. When they were almost at Lucy's house, Todd saw something.

There was yellow tape all round a lamp post. A truck was just down the road. There was an old, bashed car on its trailer.

"Don't stop," Todd's mum said to his dad. She looked scared. "Let's go to Lucy's house."

There was a police car outside the house. The front door was open. They rushed inside. Lucy's mum was crying. A police officer was trying to comfort her. Another was talking to Mr Brown.

“It was a drunk driver,” Lucy’s dad told them. “Just a lad, they say. He knocked Lucy off her bike and she hit a lamp post.”

“How is she?” Todd asked.

Mr Brown was too upset to say. Todd turned to the police officer.

“I’m her boyfriend,” Todd told him. “You’ve got to tell me. How badly hurt is she?”

"It's serious," the police officer said. "She's very badly hurt. The hospital don't know if she'll recover."

# Chapter 3
# Talk to Her

Todd missed his exam the next day. He was at the hospital. Lucy hadn't woken up. He stood by her bed with her mum.

"I feel so bad," he told Mrs Brown. "I wish I'd cycled home with her."

"The car might still have hit her," she told him. "You mustn't blame yourself. She was very happy with you."

Lucy had black bruises on her arms and a bandage on her head. There were tubes coming out of her. But she didn't look very ill. She looked asleep.

"We don't know how bad the damage is. The X-rays aren't clear," the doctor told Lucy's parents and Todd. "She might not wake up for a long time."

Todd sat with her.

“Talk to her,” the doctor said. “She might be able to hear you.”

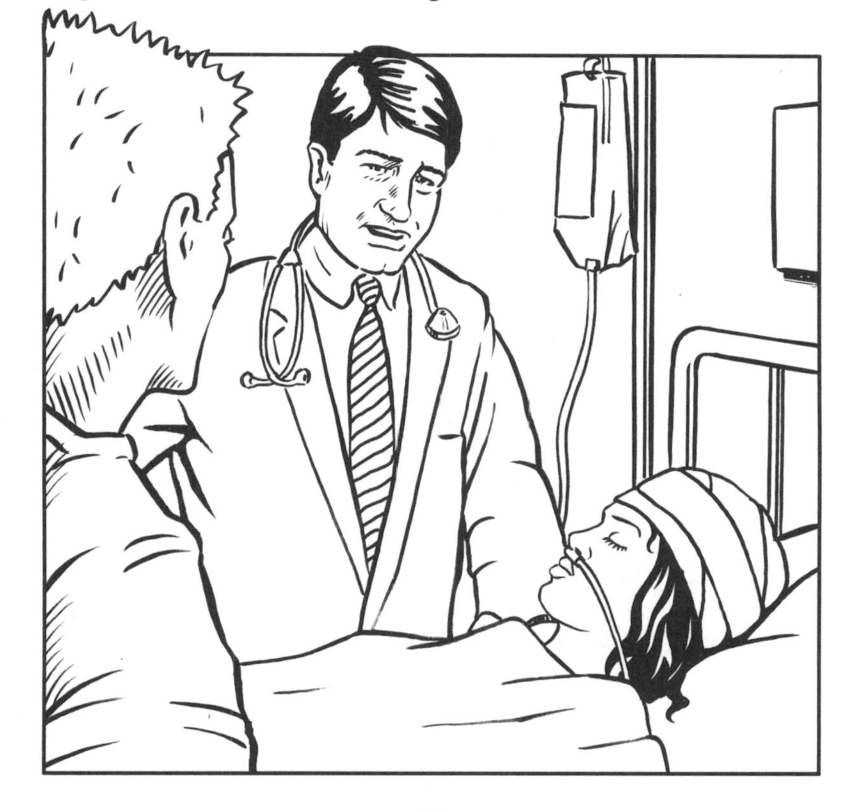

Todd tried to talk to Lucy. It was hard when her mum and dad were there. After a while, Mrs Brown went home. She had to look after Lucy's little brother. 2 hours later, Lucy's dad fell asleep. Todd told Lucy how much he loved her.

"One day this will all be in the past," he told her. "Things will be even better than before. I promise."

Lucy gave no sign that she could hear him. Her dad woke up and went to talk to the doctor.

"You look dead on your feet, Todd," he said when he came back. "I've called your mum to take you home. Our Lucy won't wake up for a while yet."

He was right. When Todd rang up that night, Lucy was still asleep. The doctors did tests on her in the morning. Todd cycled to the hospital and waited for the results.

"We still don't know if she has brain damage," the doctor said. "She may and she may not. Lucy is in a coma. We don't know how long it will be before she wakes up."

Mrs Brown began to cry. So did Mr Brown. Todd went to sit with his girlfriend. She was in a coma. A coma could last for ages. But people in a coma nearly always woke up.

Didn't they?

# Chapter 4
# Sunday Girl

Weeks went by. At first, Todd went to visit Lucy every day. Then his parents made him go to Spain with them, just for a week. When Todd got back, he went to see her every other day.

There was no change in Lucy. She looked fine. Her bruises had gone. The doctors said that they couldn't find any more internal damage. But they still had no idea when she would wake up.

It took Todd weeks to ask the most scary thing. "If she does wake up," he asked, "will she be a vegetable?"

"We don't know," said the doctor. "She may have a little brain damage. Or a lot. Or none at all. The scans don't show how much damage there is."

"Are you sure she isn't brain dead?" Todd asked.

"We're sure," the doctor said. "Our scans show that her brain is active. We hope that Lucy's brain is slowly mending itself. She'll wake up when her brain is ready."

"But how long will that be?" Todd asked.

"We have no idea," the doctor said. "It could be years."

LECTURE
ROOM

The new term began. Todd stopped going to see Lucy so often. At first he went twice a week. Then it was only Sundays.

There was lots of work to do at his new college. He had new friends to hang out with.

Most of them didn't know about Lucy. Todd was glad he didn't have to talk about his girlfriend. The story was too sad.

There was one girl at college that he really liked. Jade talked to him all the time.

She seemed to like him a lot. Todd fancied her, too. But he didn't ask Jade out. He hung out with her in a group of friends.

After a few weeks, Jade asked him to come over for Sunday dinner.

"I spend all this time with you," she said. "My parents want to meet you."

"There's something I always do on a Sunday," he said.

"Are you scared of meeting my parents?" she asked.

"No, but they'll think I'm your boyfriend."

"You *are* my boyfriend," said Jade. "Everyone at college thinks so. Aren't you?"

Todd didn't know what to say. He didn't want to hurt Jade. But he couldn't cheat on Lucy.

"OK," he said. "I'll come for dinner on Sunday."

# Chapter 5
# Do You Love Me?

The next Sunday, Todd got to the hospital early. He was alone with Lucy. She looked as lovely as ever. But there was no change. He talked to her.

"There's this girl called Jade," Todd told her. "We're good mates but she wants to be

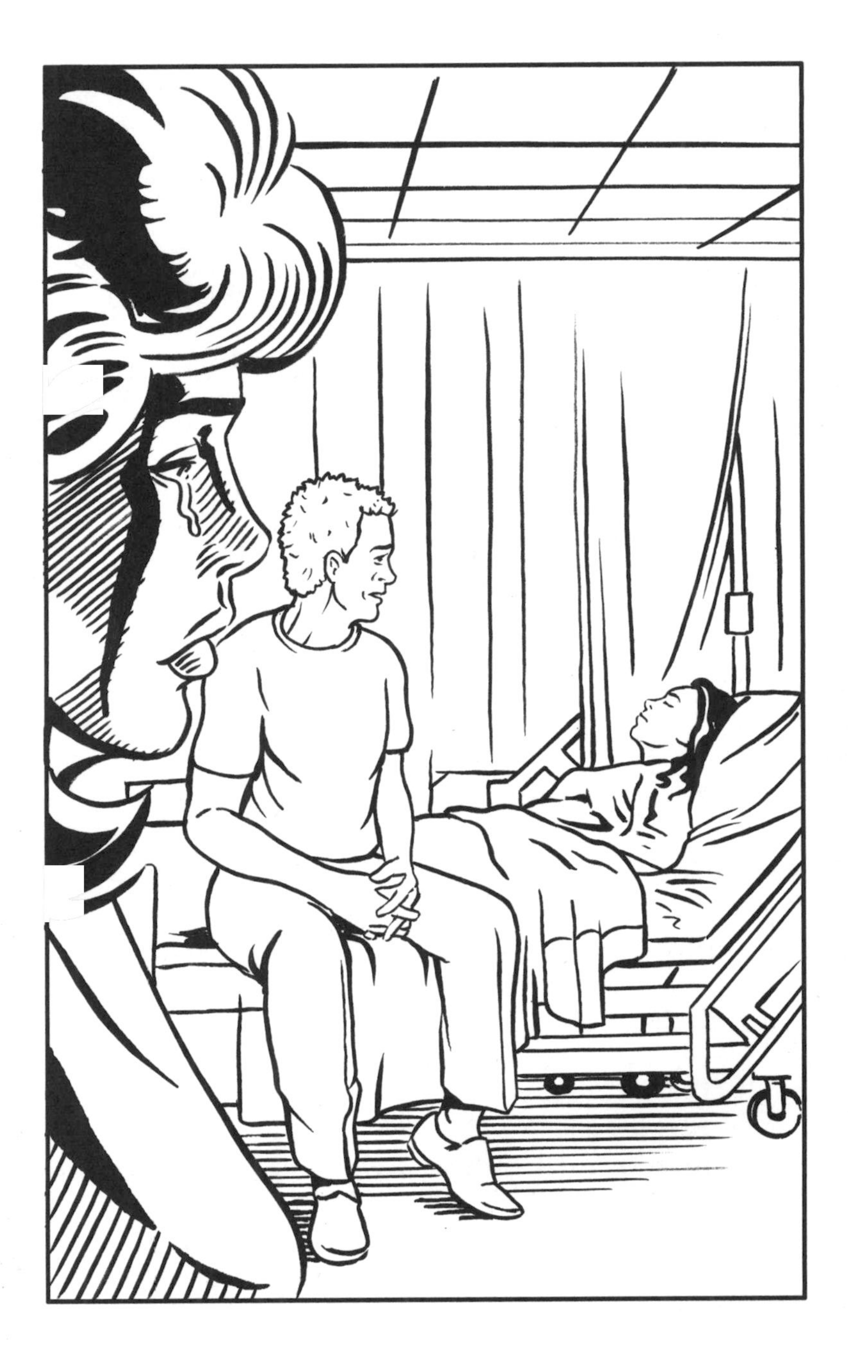

more. I don't want to hurt her. But you'll always come first, Lucy. I still love you. I miss you. I want you to understand."

He looked round. Mrs Brown had come in.

"Lucy would understand," she told Todd. "She'd want you to have a life. But promise me you'll come and see her from time to time."

"I will," Todd promised. Then he went to dinner at Jade's house.

Todd began going out with Jade. It felt good in one way, but bad in another. Todd felt he was betraying Lucy. He missed her so much, even when he was with her.

Jade was good fun. But she liked to know where Todd was all the time. She wanted to see him on Sundays.

"Where do you go every Sunday afternoon?" she asked.

"I visit the hospital," Todd said.

"Family?" she asked.

"No," he said. "An old friend."

"Not a girlfriend?"

Todd tried to explain about Lucy. Jade became upset. Todd saw that he'd made things worse by keeping it a secret.

"Are you still in love with her?" Jade asked.

“No,” Todd lied. “She’s in a coma. She’s not really alive. She may never be alive again.”

“I should finish with you,” Jade said.

“Please don’t,” Todd begged. “I need you.”

“But you like another girl more than you like me,” Jade said.

"I'll tell you what," Todd said. "Come to the hospital with me. You can see Lucy. Then you'll understand."

He expected her to say *no*.

"OK," Jade said. "I'll come."

# Chapter 6
# Kiss

They had to wait outside while the nurses washed Lucy.

"How long has she been here?" Jade asked.

"6 months," Todd said.

They went in. Todd felt odd. He couldn't talk to Lucy the way he always did. Jade got in the way.

"She's very pretty," Jade said.

Todd didn't know how to reply. "Yes," was all he said.

"I'm sure she'd understand about us," Jade said.

"I think so," Todd said. But he wasn't sure. He felt bad. Lucy was his first love.

Jade should not be here. His new girlfriend kissed him on the cheek.

"So what do you two do when you visit *every week*?" Jade asked.

"I talk to her."

"About what?"

"I tell her what I've been doing," Todd said.

"Have you told her about me?" Jade asked.

"A little," Todd said. He looked at Lucy. One of her eyes half opened. That did happen sometimes.

"Have you told her how great we are together?" Jade asked.

This made Todd feel bad. "I think today was a mistake," he said.

"No, it wasn't," Jade told him. "Now I trust you. And I still love you."

She kissed Todd. She wanted him to say he loved her. But he couldn't. Lucy's eyelids flickered.

"Did you see that?" Jade said to Todd.

"It doesn't mean anything," Todd told her.

Lucy opened both of her eyes.

"Where am I?" she said.

# Chapter 7
# Waking Up

The doctor rushed in. Lucy tried to sit up. She looked at Jade.

"Who are you?" she asked.

"I'm Todd's girlfriend," she said.

Todd swore. This was not how he wanted Lucy to find out about Jade.

"Who's Todd?" Lucy asked Jade.

Jade pointed at Todd. Lucy looked at him.

"I don't know you," she said.

"I think you'd better go now," the doctor told Todd and Jade. "We have a lot of tests to do."

"I'll call your parents," Todd told Lucy. She gave him a look that he didn't understand.

"I wonder why she woke up when she did," Jade said to Todd. "Do you think it was because of us?"

"I hope not," Todd said.

"Are you upset she didn't know you?" Jade asked.

"I am," Todd admitted. "But she *is* ill."

"You're lucky she doesn't know you," Jade told him. "You don't need a girlfriend with brain damage. You've got me."

Over the next few weeks, Todd visited Lucy a lot. She was slowly getting better. She talked the way she always did. The doctors said she'd be home soon. But Lucy still didn't remember Todd.

"Why are you here?" she asked. "I don't know you."

"You'll remember soon."

"You're Jade's boyfriend," she said. "Why do you come and not Jade?"

"You don't know Jade," Todd told her. "You know me. I used to be your boyfriend."

"Then you can come to my birthday party," Lucy said. "It's here on Friday night."

Todd had a date with Jade on Friday night. But he couldn't say *no* to Lucy.

"I'll be there," he said.

# Chapter 8

# I Forgot to Remember to Forget

"But you promised!" Jade said. "I made plans! We always go out on Friday!"

"It's Lucy's 16th birthday," Todd told her.

"She doesn't even know who you are!" Jade said. "Why do you go to see her? You're *my* boyfriend."

"I can't turn my feelings off like a tap," Todd said.

"So you still *have* feelings for her?" Jade said.

"I do," Todd told her.

"Then you'd better make up your mind," Jade said. "I'll make it easy for you. Her or me."

"I have to see Lucy on Friday," Todd told her.

"She doesn't even know who you are!" Jade yelled. "If that's how you feel, I'm finishing with you."

"OK," Todd said, and left the house.

He walked to the hospital. He had nothing better to do. When he got to her room, Lucy was alone.

"Why are you here?" she asked.

"I had a fight with Jade," he told her. "We split up."

"I'm sorry," Lucy said. "Was the fight about me?"

"Yes," Todd said. "It was."

“Is Jade jealous of me?” Lucy asked.

“She is,” Todd said. “And she’s right to be.”

Lucy sat up. She had that old, warm look in her eyes.

“Do you still want to go out with me?” she asked.

“What do you think?” Todd asked. He took a risk and kissed her. She kissed him back for a long time.

"I've started to get my memory back," Lucy said. "Do you want to go out with me again?"

"You bet," Todd said, and kissed her again. "How long have you known?"

"Quite a while," Lucy said, with laughing eyes.

"Hold on," Todd said. "Did you really forget who I was?"

"Does it matter?" Lucy said.

"Not a lot," Todd said.

They kissed each other again.

And again. **And again.** And again. **And again.** And again. **And again.** And again. **And again.** And again. **And again.** And again. **And again.** And again. **And again.** And again. **And again.** And again. **And again.** And again. **And again.** And again. **And again.** And again. **And again.** And again. **And again.** And again. **And again.** And again. And again. **And again.** And again.

**Barrington Stoke would like to thank all its readers for commenting on the manuscript before publication and in particular:**

Mrs J. Barter
Elizabeth Benson
Barbara Brown
Samantha Carney
Carol Hodgson
Christine Johnson
Matthew Littell
Grace Munns
Luke Price
Stephen Renforth
Nicola Spice
Sarah Jane Weaver

**Become a Consultant!**

Would you like to give us feedback on our titles before they are published? Contact us at the address below – we'd love to hear from you!

Barrington Stoke, Sandeman House, Trunk's Close,
55 High Street, Edinburgh EH1 1SR
Tel: 0131 557 2020 Fax: 0131 557 6060
E-mail: info@barringtonstoke.co.uk
Website: www.barringtonstoke.co.uk